# Puss in Boots

illustrated by Jess Stockham

**Child's Play (International) Ltd**
Swindon          Auburn ME          Sydney
© 2007 Child's Play (International) Ltd     Printed in China
ISBN 978-1-84643-075-6
1 3 5 7 9 10 8 6 4 2
www.childs-play.com

There was once a poor miller, who had three sons.

When he died, he left his mill to his eldest son, and his donkey to his second son. All that was left for the miller's youngest son was his cat.

The third son was sad. "How can a cat help me to earn my living?" he asked.

The cat came and rubbed against his knee. "You'd be surprised," he purred. "All I need is a large bag and a pair of boots." So the youngest son borrowed boots and a bag from his brothers. Puss put on the boots and walked out into the fields, carrying the bag.

He put two carrots in the bag, and pretended to fall asleep. Before long, a rabbit came along, drawn by the scent of the carrots.

As soon as it hopped into the bag,
Puss pulled the string and trapped the rabbit.

Puss went straight
to the king's palace,
and demanded
to see the king.

He bowed low, and said,
"Your Highness, I bring you
a rabbit as a gift from my master."
"And who may he be?" asked the king.
"The Prince of Carabas," the cat pretended.
"Thank him very much indeed!"
replied the king.  "I adore rabbit pie!"

Two days later, Puss went out to the fields again.
He left the bag open, with grain inside, and hid
until two pigeons flew in. He took the pigeons
to the king, as before.
"Please thank your master!" said the king.
"Pigeon pie, yum!"

Every few days, the cat would visit the king
in this way. The king wondered about the
Prince of Carabas, who was such a good hunter.

One day, Puss saw the king and his daughter driving along the road by the river.
He dashed straight home to tell his master.
"Quickly!" he miaowed. "Time for a swim! Hurry!"

As soon as his master was in the river, Puss hid his clothes and ran in front of the king's carriage.

"Help!" he cried "My master, the Prince of Carabas, is drowning!" The young man was very surprised to be dragged out of the water!

"Robbers have stolen my master's clothes,"
Puss pretended, "and thrown him in the river!"

"No problem!" said the king. "There are plenty
of clothes at my palace." And he sent one
of his servants to fetch a fine suit.

"We are having a little drive," explained the king. "Won't you join us?"

The young man was puzzled
by the king's kindness, but he readily agreed.

Meanwhile, Puss ran on ahead, and came across some villagers working in the fields. "The king is coming," he told them. "If he should ask, you must tell him that the Prince of Carabas owns these fields!"

Sure enough, the king's carriage came to a stop. The princess and the young man did not notice, for they were deep in conversation. The king asked the villagers who owned the fields.

"Why, your Majesty, it is the Prince of Carabas!" "Indeed!" he replied. "These are fine fields."

Meanwhile, the cat ran on ahead, and came
across some more villagers working in the woods.
"The king is coming," he told them.
"If he should ask, you must tell him that
the Prince of Carabas owns these woods!"

Sure enough, the king's carriage came to a stop.
The princess and the young man did not notice,
for they were deep in conversation. The king
asked the villagers who owned the woods.

"Why, your Majesty, it is the Prince of Carabas!"
"Indeed!" he replied. "These are fine woods."

Meanwhile, the cat ran on ahead, until he came
to a large castle on top of a hill, surrounded
by many fields and forests.  He knocked
on the gates, and asked to speak with the master.

In the castle lived an old magician,
who was very mean to his servants.
"A cat in boots!" he laughed.
"Send him up! I am a little hungry,
so he may stay longer than he would like!"

Puss was terrified, but he refused to show it.
"I don't believe you can do magic," he said.
"They say you can turn yourself
into any animal you want, but it can't be true!"
"Really?" answered the wizard.
"Pick an animal, and I will show you!"
"A lion," purred the cat.
"One that's about
to have dinner,"
he added quickly.

In a flash, the wizard turned into a fierce lion,
and behind him there appeared a huge feast!

"It must be harder to change yourself into a small animal," continued Puss. "Like a mouse, say."
"Easy!" snarled the lion, and instantly became a tiny mouse. The cat jumped on him at once – and that was the end of the wizard! The servants were delighted.

"Just in time!" thought the cat, as he heard the noise of the king's carriage coming up the drive. "Welcome to the home of the Prince of Carabas, your Highness!" he said. "Dinner is served."

The king, the princess and the young man
sat down at the long table, which was laden with pies
and cakes and meat and fruit. They did not
finish eating until they were absolutely full.

"This is the best time I've had all year!" said the king.
"I hope we will be able to visit again."
"Won't you join us?" the princess asked the cat.
"Thank you, Princess," miaowed Puss,
"but I've already eaten."

The king and his daughter often visited the castle. It was not long before the princess decided that she liked the young man so much, that there was not much point ever leaving it, and they decided to be wed. As for the cat, he had worked hard to make his master's fortune, and now he was content to rest. He sat every day in the full sun, telling the kittens long stories about how wizards could turn into mice, and millers into princes!